AF624035

Love Misconstrued

Pratima Raj

FanatiXx Publication

FanatiXx® Publication
AM/56, Basanti Colony, Rourkela 769012, Odisha
ISO 9001:2015 Certified

© Copyright, 2025 Pratima Raj

All rights reserved. No part of this book may be reproduced, stored in a retrieval system, or transmitted, in any form by any means, electronic, mechanical, magnetic, optical, chemical, manual, photocopying, recording, or otherwise, without the prior written consent of the author.

By: Pratima Raj
ISBN: 978-93-5605-468-4
Book: Love Misconstrued
Price: INR 199/-

Printing By: BooksClub.in
The opinions/ contents expressed in this book are the sole of the author and do not represent the opinions/ stands/ thoughts of FanatiXx® or any of its associates and affiliations.

Acknowledgement

The Journey of a writer commences by penning thoughts and catering to the needs of the readers.

I am thankful to all my readers for trusting me and my work; and being considerate in sharing their valuable time to read my books - Cocktales, Virgin Mother, The Colostrum, and Love Misconstrued.

It is said that opportunities knock the fortune door only once; and I am fortunate to welcome it each time it does; through the vision of my husband P. Sivasubramaniam who has always believed in my talent of becoming a profound author. I am very thankful to him for being such a supportive life-partner.

I am thankful to the almighty to bestow me with two understanding children- Kanishka and Karan, who have always been inspired by my writing skills. It's their motivation that made me pen thoughts in various genre. They rendered me the space I had required to explore in the writing field.

I extend my gratitude to my parents, sibling, well- wishers, friends, and mentors. They had always patted my back in pride and rendered trust in my talent.

God sent his angels to assist me in accomplishing my objectives in the right pathway, and so, I thank FanatiXx Publication, to embrace my work by bestowing beautiful souls- Mr. Hemant Bansal, Mr. Akshat Lakhe, Ms. Ishika Bhardwaj, Ms. Noorleen Kaur Bhatia, Ms. Saizal Gupta, and Mr. Abhijeet Ghosh for their support and guidance in assisting me to publish my book successfully.

Contents

NATASHA

"Karthik! It's been 2 years since our live-in; so, when are you planning to inform your parents about us?" I confronted Karthik.

Karthik couldn't hear me as his earphones were plugged in and I was screaming my lungs out to be heard from the kitchen, while he was seated on the couch in the hall. He was attending his online seminar. I marched towards him and stood in front with my eyes wide looking at him; while I placed my hands on my hips. He could sense that I'm anxious about something; so, to divert my attention he was trying all sorts of mischievous things like – winking; giving me a flying kiss; held my hand and pulled me to sit on his lap. Luckily, the camera was off, and the audio was muted. When I got up from his lap, he called me- "Hey, Pookie; why are you such a cutie?" He grinned for his own cringe dialogue; then he asked, "What's wrong? Why are you in a wild mood today? Come on, give me a kiss. I'll finish my seminar within five minutes, and you have me thereafter." I blushed the moment he called me Pookie. But it wasn't the time and moment to slip from my furious mode and mood. The fact is undeniable that my man knows how to calm me down, instantly!

Hi! I'm Natasha Chatterjee, a 27-year-old girl from Kolkata. I shifted to Mumbai to pursue my Master's degree; and now, have successfully completed my course. Speaking about my features, well… I'm 5 feet 4 inches tall; fair and soft skin, with long golden streaks of tresses. I'm a Bengali hailing from Kolkata; and have lived in a joint family since my childhood days till my graduation.

I am officially a fashionista now; I own a boutique at Navi Mumbai. Well, speaking about my work experience, I have worked as an intern in one of the famous fashion designer's studios for three years. Now, let me walk you through my family history. Three generations live together in the same house- My grandparents, parents and my sister. Bipasha, my younger sister, is pursuing her Doctorate in Microbiology. She is placid in nature, and an intellectual too. In short, I'm just the opposite to her. She shares the same features as me; but, with a little change. She has a short curly charcoal texture of locks, but I have long and straight tresses. Prior, I had my hair black in color; but, once, I shifted to Mumbai, I had colored it to golden streaks. Let's start the introduction journey with the lady of the house- my Mother India; Sheetal Chatterjee; she is an English professor in a college at Kolkata. I share my mother's inheritance- Bold, talkative, short-tempered and dedicated personality. My Father, Mr. Dheeraj Chatterjee, is the Principal in a Government School, at Kolkata. He is my Hero. Though Bipasha and Baba share the same qualities, he is much closer to me. He has given both the girls the liberty to speak openly on any topic; even about our personal stuff. Well, I don't hesitate, I candidly pour out my heart; but Bipasha hasn't learned to open. She does share her thoughts with Maa, at times. Next, speaking about the head of the family; my grandfather, Mr. Bankim Sanjoy Chatterjee; he is a retired Army man. He owns his disciplinary lifestyle. Morning and evening walks; timely attendance at the dining table for supper. Though, he is a changed man now. He helps Baba in his day-to-day tasks like paying bills, purchasing vegetables, gardening and assisting my grandmother, Mrs. Sushma Mouhima Chatterjee, in cleaning the greens, chopping them too, sometimes. We all have a hectic schedule at home; and when we have the sharing hands, life and work becomes easy, and bonds are made stronger.

Now, getting back to the scenario, where I was furious with Karthik for taking our relationship for granted. I packed my bag and left home without cooking any meal for that day. Karthik was still in his seminar, and I gave him a stern look, while taking the car key. I had stuck a note for him on the fridge informing – "No Meal Today!"

Karthik called me as soon as he had finished his session- "Hey, Nat! What's wrong? Why didn't you cook today? You were giving me a dead stare, while I was in my session; Why?"

Before I respond to his query, let me introduce you to my boyfriend- Karthik Suraj Batliwalla. He is a Businessman. He joined his father's business after his post-graduation. They deal in Import and Export of Gemstones and Jewelry. He is a Gujarati and settled in Mumbai. He is 27 years old; and 5 feet 9 inches tall, with beautiful features. He is fair and handsome too; with blue eyes, and silky black hair. I have always requested him to color his hair to look even more appealing, but he refrains. Karthik gives a vibe of a Macho man - Bold, Gym body, smart, tall; and added to his personality is his beautiful nature like - jovial, cute, caring and diplomatic. He is a mature person who doesn't believe in acting impulsively. He takes his time to analyze things and then brings it to action. This quality of his, I adore a lot. But what annoys me a lot about him is that he drags it till the last minute, rendering perplexity. Well, coming back to the issue; I am mad at him; as he hasn't spoken to his parents about us for the past two years, despite reminding him. He promises to do so, but all my efforts go in vain. It's every girl's insecurity when engaged in a relationship and it's normal to feel this way; but this guy doesn't give a shit. I don't understand one thing about him - when he is so sure about our relationship, then what's stopping him from giving assurance, in the name of commitment? I'm not asking him to marry me immediately; but to involve the parents from both ends; to keep them in the loop and not to bother about our future settlement.

Coming back to the moment where Karthik is calling me and I am answering his call.

"Hello…What do you want, Karthik? When I have left a note saying no meal, then what makes you call? I'm driving!

"Hey, Nat! What's wrong? What did I do? Why are you mad at me? "

"When are you going to speak to your parents about us?"

"I will! Give me some time. Why hurry?"

"Oh Yeah! Why hurry? My mother is looking for a groom for me; and I am tired of making excuses to her."

"Fine, Sweetheart! I will speak about us by next week."

"Karthik…., my mom is calling me. I must go through the same topic again. All thanks to you."

Before Karthik could say anything, I hung up his call abruptly.

The moment I hung up; my mother called- “Natasha…why was your call engaged for so long? All good?”

“Yes, Maa! I was talking to my assistant regarding a client’s assignment for the upcoming event. What happened, Maa? Is everything fine?”

“Yes, Beta! All good! I have been sending you so many profiles of grooms, but you have not yet updated me on any?”

“I have lots of work, so no time!”

“Natasha, you are 27 years old; how long do you want me to wait? You have your younger sister too, whose future is also to be decided. People are gossiping about you.”

“Let them, Maa! Don’t bother about it! If you have searched for a groom for Bipasha and she is fine with it …go ahead and get her married, first.”

“What’s wrong with you? What are you up to, Natasha? How could I do that?”

“Nothing is wrong! I’ll call you later; I’m receiving a call from my client, bye take care.”

I hung her call to escape from further interrogation. As I drove the car on the highway; not worrying about peak traffic or signals, unlike the city; my memory flashed back to the days when I got acquainted with Karthik for the first time.

Karthik and I studied in the same college at Mumbai, but in different genres. He was pursuing his Master's Degree in International Business (MIB) and I was pursuing a Master's Degree in designing (M. Des in Fashion Designing). We met at a mutual friend's party. I was standing across from him, and he was glaring at me frequently, while talking to his friends; making an awkward situation for me.

Karthik has a charismatic personality. Most of the girls in our college have a crush on him. They would flirt with him equally as he would do with them. My best friend Kavita noticed him gazing at me. She expelled a grin and asked me- "Nat! I think someone is very interested in you? Since, the moment we have joined this party, that guy, who is wearing black shirt and Jeans with two buttons open showing his broad, clean shaved chest, is staring at you." Said Kavita pointing her fingers towards Karthik.

"Bullshit! Don't assume or overthink any crap, Kavitha!"

"Okay. Cool! I'm just kidding! I'm going for a refill of my drink; do you want anything?"

"No! I'm good! Come fast!"

"Okayyyyyy…."

Karthik notices me alone; and so, he picks up his glass of wine and approaches me.

"Hi! I'm Karthik!

"Hello! I'm Natasha Chatterjee!"

"Natasha, nice name!"

"Thank you."

"Natasha, why do I feel we have met before? Your face is reminiscent of someone close to me. But not sure who?"

Without entertaining any further conversation, I gave him a cold response to banish him from my sight, in a decent and indirect way.

"I don't know."

"Can I know from which department and college?

"Same college where you study; as I have seen you often in the college premises; and I'm your friend's sister's classmate."

"Fashion Designing?"

I nodded in agreement.

"Could you please excuse me now?"

I left the place, at once, after bidding goodbye to the birthday girl; and pulled Kavita along with me.

We took an auto rickshaw which was standing right outside the building. On our way to the hostel; Kavita confronted- “What’s wrong with you? Why were you behaving so cold with Karthik? He was just getting acquainted with you, that’s it!

“I’m not interested, Kavi! Neither I feel good when he’s around.”

Kavita was infuriated with my weird behavior.

Though we were seated next to each other in the auto rickshaw; we could feel a vacuum in- between; as silence was accompanying us.

It is often said that- ‘It’s written in Destiny’. Hence, I had to encounter it too. I bumped into a person again, whom I never wanted to meet. I met Karthik while I was waiting for my bus the next day.

“Hi! We meet again!”

“Yep!”

A thought crossed my mind just as a passing cloud-My bad!

I shoved a fake smile at him not knowing what to do or say next.

He broke the silence – “Can I drop you somewhere?”

“No! Thank you, my bus will be arriving anytime now.”

“I have just crossed the route, your bus will take time, due to peak traffic hours. You might get late for your lectures.”

I hesitated for a moment. Looked at my watch and realized that Karthik was right.

I walked ahead and sat on Karthik’s bike; and he rode me to the college. After a 20-minute ride, we reached college. Everyone’s eyes popped out on encountering us, together. I got down and thanked him.

“Thank you, Karthik.”

“You're Welcome!”

“Karthik…. which department?”

“You have come to your friend’s birthday party, and you don’t know your friend’s brother’s genre?”

I expelled a smile out of embarrassment.

“MIB -Master of International Business.”

I randomly asked him – "I have noticed that you seem to be very popular in college."

"Yes, I guess! People like me and I too don't mind their company."

He too found a chance to speak a bit longer to me.

"Anyways. I have observed that you are reserved, an introvert! Am I right?"

"Not exactly! I'm an extrovert with my close friends and family members."

"So…friends?"

A thought passed by while he was waiting for my response- Natasha, he is asking you to befriend him and not for a date. So, let's keep the delusional world to a halt.

I expelled a smile at him, as a response. Neither a Yes nor a No is the answer, for now. He is so charismatic that any girl would fall for him or instantly befriend him; but I must maintain my distance with him, as I don't make friends so quickly. I usually take my own time. To escape from him, I had to make an excuse; and at once, left the place– "Ok, Bye. I'm getting late, and... thanks, once again!"

"You are welcome, again." Said Karthik, while winking at me. I was clueless as to how to react; so, I walked past my steps towards my class.

Not a few, but many times we bumped into each other. Karthik's transition of becoming- 'Just a friend' to something more; was visible by his action; he started 'following' my Instagram and Facebook accounts. Though, I have taken some time to follow him back on social media, I would stalk him whenever I was online. He has a strong profile with a huge number of followers. His posts were very interesting. Some were with friends; either at a party or somewhere out of town; mostly, Goa, Jammu and Kashmir, and Bike ride to Leh. I had the chance to peek into his personal picture on his highlight section of Instagram page. There was a picture where he is seen clinking glasses of whiskey with an elderly man of around 50 years old with the caption – 'World's best person!' I assumed; he must be his father.

Thereafter, we met frequently from the day he gave me a lift; either at my favorite café, just outside the college premises or at the college canteen. I learnt that he too likes listening to old Bollywood songs of the 90s, as I do. We hummed a few songs too, on our way to college. Our acquaintance turned to friendship. *Cupid's[1] love conspiracy was to strike the arrow in our hearts, and it was a success too. We fell in love. Oh. Sorry; correction; we were rising in love. Rising in the sense, we made sure we weren't a hindrance on each other's path of life. Neither did we envied one another's achievements; nor controlled each other; Instead, we celebrated our small wins.

Since the time I joined the college, I have been accommodated in the ladies hostel. I wasn't comfortable there, though, as hostel food and life were draining my interest from college. Day and Night only one place to roam around. How boring, isn't it? I am an explorer. I love exploring places and food. Yes, I am a foodie; you read me right. Hence, I decided to stay with Kavita from thereon. Kavita too wanted a roommate for her. She lives as a Paying Guest, at her relative's bungalow, located 5 Kms away from college.

The next day, I packed all my belongings and informed the warden about my checkout from the hostel. I had informed my parents too, about the shift. The moment I reached Kavita's place; I paid an advance deposit to the house owner; and started enjoying my stay and company with Kavita.

[1] Cupid – Roman God of Love.

We would watch movies late at night; help each other with chores; and cook too.

Hardly, I have lived for six months with Kavita, when I had to shift again. But this time it was to an apartment. Kavita was upset about the decision but was very understanding. Hence, no resentments.

Karthik and I are in a relationship now. Karthik wanted me to shift to his apartment, and I too agreed to his decision; as we both wanted to accept the odds; the good and the flaws; and it was possible, only when we lived together. Yes, It's a "Live-in!"

AT THE APARTMENT

Karthik, as a responsible boyfriend, picked me up from Kavita's house; and helped me carry my belongings to the car and placed it in the boot. Then, I bid adieu to my bestie; tears unwilling to control its fall from my eyes and landed upon my cheeks. Hence, the effect of FOMO (Fear of Missing Out). It's not that I won't be meeting Kavita, at all. We belong to the same FD (Fashion Designing) department. But still, girls' bond can never be explained; it's exceptionally different and beautiful in its own way.

On our way to Karthik's place; he played some songs to divert my mind. He sang the song played from the radio; and for sure he gave me a vibe of a bathroom singer. He cracked some silly jokes too. He pulled out some tissue paper from his car's storage area and gave it to me. I must say, he has a knack for taming the whispers of the storm; and this quality of his I am really in love with. We spoke about my family and my native place. In-between college topics too was on our discussion list; and finally, we reached his place.

Worli, at Mumbai, is known for its beautiful scenic view of Arabian Sea, along with the sea link- a Cable bridge between

Bandra and Worli. An Apartment here is a dream of many, and I couldn't take my eyes off the building which was 22 floors high. The entrance was at its best. Security Check of every vehicle was tight; and once you have cleared the procedure, the check post barrier opens for the vehicle to pass. The charismatic landscape was a visionary treat. Karthik did not disturb me from my moment.

He pulled a smile when our eyes hooked. We reached our parking lot and parked the car. We carried our belongings and headed towards the lift.

I didn't turn towards Karthik, even once, while heading towards the building elevator, as I was cherishing the scenic pleasure and the aura of the place. We entered the building, and he pressed the button; the lift opened its twin doors. We placed our baggage inside the elevator; and to my astonishment, he pressed the button to the 22nd floor. It gave me goosebumps, on the feeling of living at the top of the building-Just like- the feeling of being at the top of the World. It made me speechless. Karthik broke the silence – "Hey cutie, speak up! I have been noticing you for quite some time, you are lost. Is everything okay?"

"Karthikkkkkk! I'm in a dream world. Nothing seems to be real."

Karthik guffawed. I have never seen him so happy. People guffaw, when they are in glee. We locked our eyes, embracing the silence between us in a romantic mode. Before the magnetic pull did its work, we reached the floor. We unloaded the luggage from the lift. He searched for his key from his bag, and finally, unlocked the door.

I walked past the hallway of the house, where I encountered beautiful wall mounted hand paintings around. Some expensive home decor was kept at every nook and corner of the house too. There was a beautiful chandelier hanging at the center of the room. To my left, there was a small round-shaped table with the two chairs, in the dining hall; with an open kitchen. To my right, there was a sofa set placed with a glass center table; and a big television, been wall mounted; the hall has a balcony with lots of plants and a green carpet placed with two chairs and a small table, giving me a vibe- at dawn, chai time mode; and at dusk, cheers mood. Meanwhile, Karthik got me a glass of chilled ice-cold water. When he opened his fridge, to get some fruits out; I encountered crates of beer cans, occupying most of the space; while some fruits and veggies too, had done their duty of filling the fridge. When Karthik opened his freezer compartment, I was surprised to see an unusual thing which normally boys don’t encourage to stuff it in their fridge; and that was *Cassata* Ice- cream.

“Here... have this; it will cool you down!”

“Thank you, baby!”

“Karthik, I didn’t know that you like Cassata Ice-cream.”

“Baby…I love both; Natasha and Cassata.” He pulled me towards him and kissed me.

“Chee. How cringey!

Then, he blindfolded me, once I was done quenching my thirst. He held my hand and headed towards a small pathway; with my other hand I could feel the wall. “Karthik... Where are you taking me?”

“Shhhhh...Silence, Sweetie! You will know soon.”

I could sense that Karthik was trying to open the doorknob. Once, I was led into a room, Karthik released me from his hold; and untied the blinds. I opened my eyes slowly. It was blurry initially, but whatever I could take in, it was heaven.

Big King size bed with a flower vase on one side of the side table; and a light lamp on the other. As my vision got cleared, I was awestruck by the picturesque sight. A broad and tall window made the room look big and appealing with a windowsill on the interior of the room. I could imagine having the best of the time seated with a good romantic book in hand, or with Karthik (shirtless); and I, with a silky-smooth nightgown, spending our sunrise moment with a deep passionate kiss; as the outer world of the room was even more romantic and scenic in view. The vast blue sky above; and a deep dark blue sea below; with the ship sailing at a distance; and the seagulls hovering around the mid sea to catch its prey; while the breeze whistling in my ears, provoking an emotion within, as if, a boyfriend is erotically teasing his girl. There was another room, just opposite ours. I opened the door and witnessed all the gym equipment placed in one corner of the room; along with different sizes of dumbbells. There is a Queen Size bed too with an attached bathroom to it. I assume it to be the guest room and his work out room. It has a wide window connecting to the city side view- tall office buildings, and some residential apartments; along with the sound of the hustle and bustle of the big city.

Karthik and I, started living as a couple; with exchanged duties of the house chores along with cooking. I have made it clear at the beginning, to Karthik about the hygiene and tidiness to be maintained like- timely shower before getting on the bed or touching food items; as I have Mysophobia. I get anxiety issues if I see dirt, or uncovered food kept on the table or fridge, pests running around the house like rats, lizards, and cockroaches. He has been very cooperative in every way. We did our respective works; whether it was our college assignments; him assisting his father in their business; I, working out business plans for my boutique; designing customized dresses for my customers; as a part time job in a fashion studio. We have gifted the required space and time to one another.

Days passed bye; and we were turning 1.5 years old in our relationship. Everything between us was moving perfectly. We have adopted one new addiction in our life and that was to regularize walking; and we opted for the night walks at the seashore. We desire to spend the beautiful moments together alone, away from the crowd, and hence, would visit the shore around 10 pm; with the gleaming huge white ball at the night; sounds of the erratic waves gushing against the rock; twinkling stars at the dark sky; and we holding hands on the beach side. Post walking, we would have our weak moments too. Not too engrossed though; just a wild yet mild passionate kiss and cuddles. I, at times, would engrave our names on the wet sand; but the envious waves would wash it away. While I'm busy playing with the sand, Karthik would admire the child in me, and grin. We would spend a minimum of two hours on the shore. Once done with our activities, we would walk back home and drop off asleep.

The next day, it was my birthday. I, for the very first time, forgot about it. Karthik made breakfast; and brought it to the room while waking me up. I was clueless about the act, as it was a Friday; and Fridays are my turn to cook. Then, he placed a candle on a piece of cheesecake and wished me. We had our hot beverage and breakfast in our room seated on the windowsill admiring the scenic view.

"Thank you, baby; for this surprise! This morning is perfect." I planted a kiss on his cheeks.

Karthik pulled out a box from his pocket and handed it to me. It was a solitaire Ring.

"Happy birthday, Love!" He wished me by brushing his lips against mine.

I was awestruck by the beauty of it; but I was not ready to accept such an expensive gift.

"Thank you, Karthik, but I can't take such an expensive gift, it's not right."

"Sweetheart, Chill! Please, I insist!"

I made up my mind to own it, after Karthik's continuous efforts to convince me. Then, once I got freshened up; I wore the ring and asked Karthik to drive me to the Kali Mandir; to pray for our final semester; before attending our lecturers. We

Bengalis believe and pray to Goddess Kali. After the prayers were done, while driving towards our college I informed Karthik about my evening schedule.

"Karthik, I will make a visit to Mansukh Bhai's tailoring shop, in the evening. I have given my dress for stitching. I had designed it for my birthday and wished to wear it today. I will reach home on time, don't worry."

"Okay, babe!"

We reached college and to our respective departments. Kavita greeted me –

"Happy Birthday, Natasha!"

She hugged me. She noticed the solitaire ring on my finger.

"OMG! Don't tell me, Karthik gifted you this on your birthday?"

"Yes!" I blushed.

"Wow. He proposed to you; Lucky girl!"

"No! He just wished me and gave me this."

"Are you guys in a Situationship?"

"What? I didn't get you. What's Situationship?"

“You really don’t know? I thought you both have mutual consents.”

The professor entered the class and headed with the topic. For an hour I was physically present there, but mentally absent.

Once, the bell rang and there was a break for 10 minutes. I rushed to Kavita and asked her to explain the word, Situationship!

“Tell me Kavi, what was that you were about to tell me about Situationship?”

“Situationship is between two people who love each other and live together, but don't want to label their relationship. They don’t want any commitments, neither want to leave one another.”

“What nonsense? I haven’t heard of this?”

“This is Gen Z Lifestyle!”

“Karthik is not like this. I know him. I will ask him to speak about us to his parents right away.”

“Not today, Nat! It’s your special day, don’t spoil your mood.”

“Okay.”

The day in the college got over and I proceeded to the tailor shop as planned. Out of the blue it started raining. Mumbai rains were unpredictable. It poured so heavily that there were huge traffic jams due to waterlogging issues. I waited in my auto rickshaw for half-an hour and when the route got cleared, we were moving at a sloth's pace. Finally, I reached the shop. I paid the auto driver and met Mansukh Bhai.

“Namaste Mansukh Bhai! Mera dress ready ho gaya?”

“Haan, Madam!”

He called out to his boy and asked him to get the dress from the store. I tried it in the dressing room and found it to be unfit. I changed my attire back to what I was wearing and gave the dress to the tailor.

“Kya Bhaiya? Kaise banaya hai? Sab deela hai. Mujhe yeh dress aaj pehena hai. Abhi teekh karke do. Mein wait karungi.”

I asked the tailor to alter my dress and informed him that I will wait in the shop till it is done, as I have to wear it today.

While I was waiting for the dress, I opened my folder in my phone where I had saved the picture of the dress designed by me. Kavita had an eye on this dress; I could sense it the way she was looking at it when I showed her my design. The dress was made of satin material with a netted arm on one side; the other side was to be left sleeveless. A bow at the back. A long dazzling black gown. All day long, I was dreaming about my attire and the accessories matching with it. The tailor diverted me from my imaginary world.

"Madam, ho gaya! Phir se check kar lijiye!"

I got the dress, and re-tried it in the changing room. Everything was perfect. I paid Mansukh Bhai and hired a taxi. It was 8 pm, and I forgot to message Karthik about the delay. I pulled out my phone from my bag, and messaged him, while on the drive. "Hi, Karthik. I am on my way back home. Sorry for the delay."

There were two blue tick signs indicating that Karthik had read my message. On the way, I recollected all the conversations in my mind which I had with Kavita this morning. Fear engulfed my mind, putting me into an anxious state, where the future of our relationship is unknown; that I could be betrayed at any moment or overthinking has brought me to such a doubtful mode? I was brought to consciousness from my thoughts, when the driver called me out loud.

"Madam. We have reached your destination."

I paid him and walked past my steps towards the elevator and reached home. The moment I reached and stood in front of the door, I gave a pep talk to motivate and cheer myself up - Natasha, calm down and enjoy your birthday evening; and keep the discussion with Karthik for tomorrow.

I took out my spare key and tried to unlock it, but it was already kept unlocked. I walked through the aisle; it was pitch dark. I switched on my phone's flashlight and reached the hall. To my surprise, the room was aromatic and pleasantly decorated with candles and rose carpet was laid towards the bedroom direction. I called out Karthik- "Karthik…."

No response. Again, I called him out – "Karthik. Where are you?" The house has been decorated so beautifully; thank you! Now come out please."

I entered our bedroom escorted by aromatic candles and rose petals laid on the walkway; and some fell on me from the fan's rotation. There was a packet on the bed wrapped with a golden cover. As I picked the gift, there was a note-

"You will look freaking hot in this attire, my Pookie! Please wear this. Love you. Waiting for you on the terrace; come soon!"

I decided to wear the dress gifted by Karthik to make him feel loved. So, I got into unwrapping the cover. I was awestruck with the design of the dress. Karthik knew that Black is my favorite color; and so, he chose the same. I went to the washroom, had a shower and put on my attire. I came out to the dressing table, blow dried my hair, put some makeup on but with no accessories, only the solitaire ring on my finger.

I climbed up the floor and entered the terrace area, which was ready with a table and two chairs; decorated with a red velvet tablecloth with lighted candles; a Chocolate truffle cake at the center; and a bottle of Champaign. This scenario reminded me of a famous Bollywood movie of the 90s; where a GF and BF meet on the terrace. On this very thought, I got overwhelmed. Karthik was standing in the dark and the moment he heard my footsteps; he came to the limelight of the frame in front of the candle flame. He got so mesmerized with my look; maybe I was so gratifying physically, that he couldn't take his sight away from me. His facial expressions said it all! His eyes and smile conveyed it loud and clear. He hooked his eye on me as if he hadn't met me before. I think I was looking very sensuous in this attire.

I broke the silence between us- "Hi!"

"Hot!"

"Hah… What?"

"You look Hot, Baby!"

"Thank you, for all this, Karthik. It means a lot."

He kept his finger on my lips, and gently touched, feeling the curve of it; and brushed his lips against mine. We were lost in each other for a moment. It was so breezy that the wind was forcing its entry towards Karthik's direction that it was pushing him towards me. The candles were put off due to the wind, but the gleaming moonlight gave us the light to see each other, madly in love. Karthik's hands rubbed against my silky dress on my waist, admiring my curves. I gently shoved him away and walked towards the edge; as I was moving towards the weak moment.

On seeing my silhouette; Karthik came near, embraced me from behind and whispered on my ears –

"Natasha! You are mine; forever!"

He, then, turned me around to face him and said- "God, has taken his own beautiful time to create you, only for me!" I got lost in his masculine voice and overwhelming words. I hooked my eyes on him, when he carried me in his arms till the table and lit the candles again; and made me cut the cake. We fed the cake to each other. Champaign was poured in the glasses, and we raised the toast. Once, we finished three rounds of our drink; and the liquid performing its duty within; Karthik, neared me, and blindfolded me. He carried me in his arms again and took me to our bedroom. He placed me on the bed and locked the room. The air conditioner's temperature was so cold that a normal human being would freeze, but I was sweating at this moment. My love, and my heartthrob, was on the mission of pacing my heartbeat; where the hot waves from the body were burning me, each time he touched me; beautifying my body parts.

For, this time, it was the most uncontrollable moment for us. We were officially, two bodies and one soul. Prior, we just had a good cuddling and kissing with some boundaries to it. But, today, this boundary was broken, just like the tsunami broke open all the barriers and engulfed everything.

The food, which was bought, was kept inside the fridge, to be consumed the next day; and we dropped off to sleep.

The next morning, I woke up late. I was still on my bed, reminiscing about last night's moments in my memory lane, which was now, a fond memory and a wow moment. Karthik had left for college. I took a day off from my classes. I walked past my steps towards the kitchen, re-heated the food and had my breakfast. I wasn't alone seated on the dining chair; I was accompanied by the flashback of conversation between Kavita and I, which was running in my subconscious mind. I decided to confront Karthik this evening without any further delay.

The Confrontation

Karthik reached home in the evening. I was busy with my assignment so I couldn't notice. After a few minutes, I walked out of my room to quench my thirst and munch something; when I encountered him. He sat on the couch with his laptop open. I walked towards him with the thought in my mind –"If not Now; then Never!"

I stood right in front of him.

"Hi, Nat! How are you, baby? You were in a deep sleep this morning, so I didn't want to disturb you."

"Thanks!"

"What's wrong? Why are you sounding so cold?

"Karthik...Do you really love me?"

"Of course! What kind of question is this?"

"Then, why aren't you speaking about us to your parents?"

"Why are you in such a rush, Natasha? Everything is going well between us, isn't it?"

"I want a commitment from you. I am not asking you to marry me tomorrow, but our parents should know about us. We are done with our final exams by this week; and now my parents want me to settle down. They keep sending me profiles of the boys from the matrimony site; and I am tired of making excuses."

"Then go ahead. Get married. Who is stopping you?"

"Karthik? Then, what was that we had last night?"

I continued. "Just a one-night stand or you are planning a Situationship?"

"You are overthinking Natasha. Calm down. You know it very well, that I want you as much as you want me. We are a perfect couple without any formalities."

"Excuse me! Want and Need have two different meanings. 'Need' involves love; whereas 'Want' manifests desire. Now you decide, what's your take on this?"

"What's wrong with you, Nat? We are about to finish our exams; and then, you have your dreams to be fulfilled; and I must settle in my life too. Earn so much that I could afford to render the best of luxurious life to you. Though I will be joining my father's business but will be travelling a lot for official meetings. I would hardly meet you. For now, we don't have any expectations, but later, we will be hovering over each other's life."

"Don't make vague excuses, Karthik. Say that you aren't interested in our marriage."

"No. Nothing like that."

"What is all this, Nat? We love each other, then why are you doubting?"

"Karthik, you have misconstrued love. Love doesn't mean getting intimate and living together as a couple; as a live-in; and when you lose interest, you are ready to move on easily, as if there was nothing between the two. Love has all the emotions involved like- attachment, attraction, loyalty, trust, faith, togetherness, adjustments, compassion and most important commitment."

"Don't be so dramatic. I said I WILL!"

After our argument we had our dinner in silence. I took my pillow and blanket from our bedroom and slept in the other room.

Karthik didn't utter a word, just dropped off to sleep in our bedroom.

The next day, we both drove to the college for our exam. We did not speak to each other for a week; we were aloof and had concentrated only on our on–going semester. Karthik would order the food online for us; before I could cook. I do adore all these efforts from him; but I am still disappointed that he hasn't disclosed anything about us to his parents.

On the last day of college, our juniors had arranged a farewell. We left home soon that day to attend the party. On the way, Karthik received a call from his dad, unexpectedly. He picked up his call, keeping his phone close to his ears.

"Hello. Papa. Kem Cho? Is everything fine? You normally don't call me at this hour."

"Karthik... We must travel to Qatar today. It's an evening flight; so, inform your professors."

"But. What happened?"

"Customs issue!"

"Oh, Okay! Will meet you soon."

"Fine!"

Karthik hung up the call and informed me about his visit to his dad's house and also his travel plan to Qatar. I heard it silently. We reached the college. I slammed the car door and walked towards the auditorium. Karthik had parked his car in the parking lot and walked towards the principal's room to seek leave permission for two days; and also, to inform about his absence from today's farewell party.

"May I come in sir?"

"Yes, Karthik; Please come in!"

"Sir, I need your permission to leave the college premises now and will not be able to attend college for two days; neither would I be able to be a part in today's farewell party; as I must travel with my father for a business purpose.

"Oh, no problem, Karthik. You can leave. I will inform the professors; but you will be missing your farewell party."

"Yes, sir! Thank You!

Karthik commuted back to his home; packed his stuff; and drove to his dad's home which is at Bandra.

The Travel

I reached home in the evening. I always have a spare key with me. This time, home wasn't a home; it had just mere walls and an empty space, without Karthik. I walked through all the rooms along with the ghost of memories. The flashback was running like a record player in my mind, starting from-The day I entered the apartment; the fond moments, where we cleaned the house together; and also cooked varieties of cuisines, making a mess of the kitchen; and my birthday night; that's was the cherry on the cake. Yes, arguments too. I was accumulating all the beautiful memories, when my phone lit bright indicating an incoming call. It was from my grandmother.

"Hello, Thakuma! Apani kemana achena? Is everything fine?

"Hello beta! I was missing you and I don't keep well, nowadays. I want to meet you. Is it possible for you to make a visit here?"

"Yes, Thakuma! I will book my tickets right away!" I hung up her call, then, clicked the online booking app on my phone, and booked my train ticket, right away. Thereon, I mailed my leave application to the Department, informing the cause of my visit to my home. I messaged Karthik too.

"Hi, Karthik! Thakuma isn't well; Hence, I am travelling to Kolkata tomorrow morning. I hope you have a spare key to our apartment with you."

Just like the passing cloud, I had a thought - It's good that I am taking a break, I was missing everyone at home; and needed closure from the chaotic life. A good space will bring clarity to Karthik and my life.

Without wasting any time, I packed my bag; switched off the gas regulator and closed all the windows and went off to bed. Before I dozed off, I kept an alarm for 3.30 am in the morning as my train departure time was at 6 am. I had checked my phone, before switching off the night lamp, there was no reply from Karthik; even though there was a blue tick mark shown, indicating that he had read my message.

The next morning, the alarm buzzed so loud that it gave me a heart attack. I had put it off scolding myself to keep such a weird sound as a notification for the waking alarm. I got refreshed, booked a taxi and picked up my belongings; went down to the lobby area and waited for it. My taxi had arrived on time. The driver loaded my suitcase in the boot of the car and headed towards the railway station. Again, I checked my message sent to Karthik, the result was the same- no response. I had teary eyes, but wiped it off, as I don't want to waste my emotions for an unbothered creature and decided never to pick his calls and even not to reply to his messages, thereafter.

I reached the station on time. I walked past my steps to the respective platform where my train was waiting for my arrival. The journey from Mumbai to Kolkata by train takes approx.33 hours. I boarded my train and settled in my reserved seat allotted by the railways. The journey was occupied by either reading a book, sleeping, eating, snacking, and rounds to the washroom; and the same process was repeated till I reached Kolkata, my birthplace.

I got down from the train inhaled the air of my place giving me motherly vibes and then proceeded towards the taxi stand. Got into the taxi and travelled to my home with address already informed to the driver. We (The driver and I) chit-chatted on various topics like politics, weather, my college etc. Finally, I reached home.

I unloaded my belongings from the taxi and paid him. I screamed out loud- "Thakuma, Dadaji, Maa, Baba, Bipasha; I am back!"

I entered the house's entrance; when I encountered everyone coming out from their respective rooms towards the hall to greet me. We embraced each other with tears rolling out without permission to manifest happiness. I bowed down to seek blessings from Thakuma and Dadaji. Then, I pulled my luggage to Bipasha's room; which was mine initially. Okay, fine; "Our;" as sisters' share things; that's what sister love is all about. Got refreshed and headed straight to the dining table where everyone was waiting for me to have our supper, together.

To my surprise, there were more dishes on the table. "What's this Maa? So many dishes today."

"Yes! My daughter has come home, so it's celebration time."

I opened all the lids of the bowls placed on the table. This time all were my favorites- Macher Jhol (a fish gravy); Aloo Posto (A potato dish); Shukto (Vegetarian dish); Misti Doi (Sweet flavored Curd); Roti, Mutton Biryani; and, Sandesh (A sweet made of condensed milk). We were having a good time together, after a long time; we were giggling, laughing, teasing and small, cute fights between Thakuma and Dadaji, were the added memories to this trip. I was devouring the food in a way as if encountering food for the first time. Home- cooked foods are special; and the realization arrives only when you don't get it. I over-ate so much that I wanted to go for a walk. I called Bipasha to give me company, but she had her college work;

Maa was busy cleaning the kitchen; Thakuma and Dadaji walked to their bedroom to sleep; when, my baba called me out – "Natasha, I'll join you."

I had put on my comfortable footwear and Baba too picked up his purse and phone. We walked, speaking about his work as a government school principal, his promotion, Bipasha's future and then the topic changed, speaking about my life at Mumbai, friends, studies etc. Meanwhile, Baba received a call mid of our crucial conversation. I dived into my phone to check my messages. One was from Kavita. I did not inform her about my travel plans. It read as – "Hi, Nat! All, okay? I heard from the Dean about your grandmother's health condition. How is she now? Missing you babe!"

I put a smile on my face. I replied to her message- "Hi, Kavi! Sorry, couldn't inform you. It was a sudden plan. All good here. Granny is fine now after meeting me; and I will come soon; bye babe; Miss you too."

Next, I checked Karthik's personal window. No messages from him, nor any reply. My eyes turned watery; I was hurt even more due to overthinking; when my father noticed the change in my facial expression.

"What's wrong? Why are your eyes so watery?"

"Nothing! Nothing, Baba! Just dust, due to the wind." I tried to keep my tone poised.

A few moments later, I opened up speaking candidly about relationships. I am closer to Baba in terms of discussing topics of all kinds.

The Disclosure

I wiped my tears before it rolled down my cheeks. I did take a few moments; and walked in silence. Then, I was all ready to shoot questions about relationships.

"Baba. I want to seek advice from you on relationships." "And what do you want to know?" asked Baba, pulling a sweet smile on his face.

"About you and Maa's relationship. You guys have been married for more than 30 years; and I have seen you fighting, adjusting, compromising, struggling; yet you both come back as one team, even stronger; as a happily married couple. How's that?"

"Beta, our love language is simple, adorable, understanding and at times erratic too, but intense. We are friends first. If our love becomes weak; our friendship would help us regain our connection. Even if our arguments go to the extent, we both would try to communicate it first; and then, solve it, by giving some space to think, analyze; and not jump to conclusions."

"I realized that our generation lacks compatibility. Do you agree to it?"

"Yes, Dear! Your generation lacks patience, the sense of longingness for one another, adjustments. For petty reasons they separate from each other or seek divorce. The problem of GenZ is that- they desire 90s love, but with a touch of modernization. They wish to break the stereotypes of living culture, to- Live-in; Situationship, Ghosting, Bread crumbing etc."

"Baba! How do you know all these terms? I am really surprised!"

"I was enlightened by the students of grade 11 and 12, due to an issue occurring in my school, hence, got acquainted with the terms and have brought in some strict rules and regulations."

We didn't notice that we had reached the market area where everything was available at odd hours too. We stopped by a Paan Shop (Betel leaf stuffed with ingredients of choice- either sweet or unsweet). We have the habit of chewing Paan, post dinner as it's good for digestion, boosts metabolism, for detoxification, mood enhancer, and oral health. Baba bought it for us; and I gobbled it at once; and got some packed for others at home.

On our way back home, I disclosed my feelings for Karthik to Baba, giving a short intro about him.

"Baba, I'm in a relationship with a boy named Karthik. He has pursued his MIB Degree. We studied in the same college. I met him at a friend's birthday party. He assists his father in their Gems and Jewelry business. He has left for Qatar with his father for a business emergency. I've been living for the past 2 years in his apartment."

"Does he love you?"

"Yes, Baba! He has given me this solitaire ring on my birthday." I showed my ring to Baba.

"Did he propose?"

"No!"

"What made you stay with him? And refrain from informing me or your mother?"

"Sorry, Baba. It's a mistake, I agree. I should have informed you both. It all happened so quickly that I didn't realize. We wanted to get to know each other better; hence, decided to go for a live-in!"

"Then what's the problem?" Baba interrogated in a stern voice.

"He is not committing to our relationship. Though, he is very sure about me, and wants me as his life partner; but, hesitating to inform his parents about us."

"What do you mean by want? There should be a need. You need him as well as he needs you. You should know Want is a desire and temporary; but Need is love. Need brings along- loyalty, patience, compassion, adjustments and determination to grow old together and much more for a healthy and long relationship."

I heard him silently. After a pause he continued- "Shall, I speak to Karthik and his parents about your relationship, and seek his hand for marriage?

"No! Not at all, Baba! It was Karthik who convinced me to stay with him in his apartment; and he is very sure about our relationship and so, he will do the needful. His actions will say it all, if he is really serious about me. So, he will convince his parents and bring the proposal to you."

"Okay! But I will spill the beans to your mother."

"Fine!"

We finally reached home. I realized, when my Thakuma was screaming at Baba from the entrance, for returning home so late. She wanted to chit- chat with me, but due to medication she was feeling drowsy. But Baba knows how to calm his furious mother. He took out the Paan packet from his pocket and fed her.

We all retired to our respective rooms as it was already 2am; and I was deadly tired. I changed my attire to a Night Suite and lay on my side of the cot. Bipasha was asleep, but due to the creaky noise of the restroom door, she was awakened.

"Nat! Is everything alright? I doubt your sudden visit."

"Yes, Bip! All fine. Sleep. Good night."

"I'm not sleepy now. Can we talk?"

"Yes!"

"How is it going with you? Your studies. Any boyfriend?"

"Hey! I don't have any and I'm not interested. You tell me, you seem to have one, don't you?"

"Shut up. I am tired and very sleepy. Good night."

"Haaaaa…Good Night!"

Meanwhile, Baba would have spilled the beans; and I know, on hearing this, she would have been baffled. Hence, tomorrow morning would be an exclusive interrogation round with my mother.

The Drama for the Karma

The next morning, I woke up late. I dozed off as if sleeping after years. Maybe it's a sign of tranquility in my mind, and home is that serene place. I woke up around 10 am. I got refreshed and came to the dining area asking for a cup of coffee from my mother.

My mother had taken a day off as I had come. She prepared coffee and handed it to me, giving a stern look. I was aware and ready for the drama of my Karma. I strode towards the kitchen and cuddled her from behind. She moved, facing me and confronted me.

"I heard something from your Baba, last night? Is that true?"

"Yes, Maa."

"I sent you to Mumbai to live your dreams and not for a live-in!"

"Sorry!"

Thakuma joined the ladies' gang. Dadaji was seated on a sofa with his newspaper; Baba was off to school; and Bips, off to her college.

Thakuma enquired my mother about the issue. My mother narrated the whole karma of mine. On hearing this, Thakuma said- "Arey, Beta; what type of love are you dealing with, where there is no trust, no patience. Your Dadaji and I are from an old, yet golden era. We did have differences; but I made the effort to sort it out. Relationships should be taken care of by the girls only. It's our duty."

To this I replied to her- "Thakuma, in your generation, girls must bury their desires; compromise to fit in; and bow down just to save the relationship with the egoistic men. But we GenZ are different. We have equality."

"No use, speaking to you. Do what you want. You will remember my words and realize my advice, when you are in trouble." Thakuma left for her room, infuriated.

My mother's confrontation was on halt mode for a few minutes, due to Thakuma. Once she left, my mother asked me bluntly- "Are you guys, having it?"

I never expected my mother to be so candid. But still I pretended to be naïve.

“What? I didn’t get it, Maa?”

“I mean SEX!”

“Yes, we do!”

“What about safety? I hope you are taking precautions?”

“Maa, this is the problem with your generation. You guys are too judgmental. Love has been misconstrued only because of such narrow- mindedness. Love is a Universal language which also teaches us to be aware, awake and mindful. We know the consequences too. It’s not always parents’ duty to teach everything; few things have to be learnt by us as our responsibility.” I paused; then, continued- “We have our respective life apart from hovering on each other. He has his friends to hang around, he assists his dad in their business; I too have friends to be with, my personal works; I want to start a boutique, for which I have to meet people, arrange things.”

I walked to the refrigerator, opened the door, pulled out a chill bottle of water, and had a swig. Then, I explained to Maa about our routine for the day.

“Maa, we used to drive to college together in the morning hours. Evenings would be different for both. At times, he would reach home late or I would. We have shared our chores. If he cooks, I clean the house and Vice-versa. That’s also love.

Sharing equal responsibilities. During my Menstruation days, he would manage both cooking and cleaning, allowing me to rest. Hope, you are getting me right."

"Natasha, what about Karthik's mother? Does she know about your relationship?"

"Karthik, never spoke about his mother. I have no Idea."

"Oh! Then, you didn't try to find out?"

"I did. But Karthik would divert the topic."

"Now, what? How do you want to proceed with this?"

"No plans. I will reach Mumbai, pack my belongings, vacate Karthik's apartment, and shift to the Ladies' hostel back."

Maa had an anxious look on her face. "Natasha, you haven't settled in your life, yet! For the past two years you are jumping from places to places to live, and now, back to the square one- the ladies' hostel." She was cooking, but her concentration was on me and my future, as it was very limpid from her actions. She added salt to the curry again, despite adding garam masala, and I had encountered everything. Then she spoke up-

"Do you want us to speak to Karthik and his father?"

“No, Maa! If he is serious, he will bring the proposal to you, along with his father, to seek my hand for our marriage.”

I left the kitchen and reached my bedroom. I checked my calls, mails and messages, when I noticed - Karthik had just sent a thumbs up emoji for my message of visiting my Kolkata home.

I wept in silence. I took my diary out and penned my emotions.

“*Rishton ki dor itni naazuk ho gayi hai ki,*

Shabdo ke badle, emoji se hi nibayi jaa rahi hai.

This is the habit I have inculcated in me; I write my emotions out, when no means to express it out. I have been doing this since I shifted to Mumbai, as there was none to share my state of mood and thoughts.

I switched off my phone; as I was enraged with Karthik’s behavior. He never gave such mixed signals. No calls, no messages, only emoji. This immature act by him was killing me from within. I was hurt. I realized that- Breakup, renders piercing pain; and I have experienced that too, now. It’s easy to hear the word move on, but it’s the most difficult and painful experience.

Karthik

I met my dad at his mansion. He was packing his bag to leave for the airport.

"Hi, Dad! All set?"

"Yes! Have you got your passport with you?"

"Yes!"

"Let's have lunch and leave for the airport."

"Yes, please! I'm starving."

Both father and son had their supper, cooked by the chef. Suraj Batliwalla (Karthik's father) has hired a chef, and few staff; as he is a single parent; and a busy business tycoon. After their supper, their driver drove them to the Airport. Karthik broke the silence in the car, while they drove to the Airport.

"Dad! What's the issue?"

"Son, our consignment has been confiscated by the Qatar customs authority."

"But, why?"

"No idea! Once we arrive there we'll know."

My Dad looked at me and said- “Don’t worry, it won’t take much time; you can resume your college soon.”

“That’s not the problem. I have been granted permission from the principal to take leave as much as I want; as I have maintained a good attendance.”

“Then, why do you look so pale?” Dad stroked the question out of the blue.

“No! I’m absolutely fine, Dad!” I answered him by averting my gaze.

To divert his attention, I shared my thoughts of shifting back to our mansion to stay with him.

“Dad, I was thinking… I’ll rent out our Apartment at Worli and stay with you. You are living alone and must be missing out on company.”

“Who said I’m lonely? I’m very much fine. We both require our respective space. Isn’t it?”

“Yes, we do! But still; you can reconsider it.” We both laughed out loud with this remark.

“Is there a break up issue, that you are being considerate, all of a sudden?”

“No!” I, again, averted my gaze from him.

We reached the Airport. Cleared all the formalities like- the Immigration; bags check-in and boarded the flight. It was a 3 hour and 50 minutes journey on the air with unlimited beverages, snacks, meals and movies to be depended upon to pass the time.

I plugged in earbuds and played a horror movie; and Dad dropped off to sleep. After our flight took off, the air hostess breached our privacy by serving a welcome drink of choice to our respective seats.

"Black Label, please!" My dad requested his choice of drink.

"I'll have a strong Beer, thank you!"

We clinked our glasses to toast it; and cherished our moments together after a long gap.

As we were enjoying our drink, Dad spoke up- "What's wrong Karthik? Don't pretend to be naïve. You know I can sense that something is fishy; I'm your father; so, speak up.

I finally confessed my feelings for Natasha to him.

"Dad, I have loved a girl named Natasha, for the past 2 years. We graduated from the same college, but in a different genre. We met at a mutual friend's party. After about six months of our friendship, we started dating each other. I fell for her and knew that she was the one. She is a Bengali, and a beautiful soul, I must say. She is chirpy in nature. I have friends of both genders; but, when I speak to her, I don't realize my presence, nor know how the time passes-by. I had convinced her to live with me in our Worli Apartment; as in- a 'Live-in!'

My father was surprised on hearing this but maintained a poised demeanor throughout the narration. After, I had done describing my love for her he said-

"Okay, then, what's the problem? She betrayed you?"

"No, Dad; I told you that, she is a beautiful soul. I love her. We both know that we are made for each other. So many girls in the college and off the college, try to hook up with me, but I don't give a damn, as I have Natasha in my life. I have avoided contact with those girls, now."

"Then, what's the issue?"

"Natasha needs a serious commitment, now; even, when, everything is going well between us. I'm requesting her to go with the flow of life; but she isn't convinced. We both have our respective dreams to be fulfilled. We could accomplish it as we desire. She wants to start her boutique. She has completed her Fashion Designing course; and also, has finished her internship with the famous celebrity 'The Taran Kulkarni's boutique. I have asked her to concentrate on her business; and I, too, wish to join our business and help you, Dad. Learn and earn the fame and the name, with my diligence; and not be mentioned as 'The Suraj Batliwalla's son."

After, hearing me out, he said-

"It's normal behavior, son. Don't panic. Any girl who has invested her life in you, has the right to demand commitment."

He paused for a moment, as the air hostess had come over to serve our meal. He continued once she left.

"Your behavior gives a feeling of a Situationship; and not a relationship. Relationships have commitment in it. You have confessed your love for her, if it is true and forever, then, why are you so confused? Mixed signals are a red flag in any relationship. You want her in your life, but without any labels is unfair, and a cowardly act. Be brave and confess your love with assurance."

"Dad, but I don't want our history to be repeated."

"What do you mean?"

"Dad, Mom and you had a love marriage, right; then, what happened in the few years that she left us? I was hardly six years old at that time. I have observed one thing; since my young age, that love is taken for granted the moment the word 'marriage,' takes it over. And, I don't want our love to be taken for granted. I want to keep it fresh, always."

"You have misconstrued love my son. Love has simplicity; and the elegance to embrace the relationship the way it is; and not complicating it by the new trends. Love is pure and shouldn't be tagged with the terms, like- breadcrumbing, ghosting, benching, Situationship, friends with benefits. It's not love; these are fraudulent acts to mislead the person in the name of love. Love is an encyclopedia of knowledge, to preach the beings- the good and the bad; the odds and the even; the acceptance and tolerance; empathy and adjustments and much more in a relationship."

Dad continued while having his meal. "It was my fault that I couldn't give your mother time. I was too engrossed in business. Travelling, meetings etc. that she was left lonely. In spite of having you, she was aloof from me. She did her duty as a mother perfectly well; but as a husband I failed. I blame my negligence. I forgot that as a couple, we have a life too. It's not the parents' responsibilities and duties alone, that has to be fulfilled. At last, your wife will remain with you till your end. So, importance should be given to her, first. Though, other relationships shouldn't be neglected. You should have a balance in life. I'm sure you will not make these mistakes, as I have confessed my mistake to you."

We landed in Qatar. We hired a taxi and headed to the Customs office. Once we reached the office, we learnt that due to negligence of our manager in-charge, the consignment was stranded for almost 15 days. We spoke to the customs authority and cleared our goods. It did take us a day to sort the issue. And once we were done, we took our flight back to India.

Again, on our flight journey, Dad continued the same topic of our relationship.

“Karthik, this time, I will come with you to convince Natasha, to forgive you; and seek her hand for the marriage from her parents. Trust me, everything will be fine. Message her once we reach Mumbai. Request her to meet you in the café or wherever, you guys normally hangout. Don’t inform her about my presence at the café; let it be a surprise.”

“But…Dad…”

“Do what I say!”

Dad dropped off to sleep; and, I too closed my eyes to unwind. Time passed by; sleeping, and having meals and beverages. Finally, after spending 3 hours 50 minutes on the air, we reached Mumbai.

I messaged Natasha, while Dad was collecting our bags from the conveyor belt at the luggage counter.

"Hi, Baby! I'm sorry for not replying to your message. I was confused as to how to react; and also, was busy at the customs office. Will explain once we meet. When are you back from your native place? Call me once you reach Mumbai, till then I will be staying with my dad, at his mansion. I have a surprise for you; bye, my Pookie, love you."

Back To Square One

After a week's stay at my home; I packed my bag to leave for Mumbai. I have some formalities to be completed in my college, before bidding goodbye to it; and also meet Kavita too.

As I came out of my room with my belongings, I met Thakuma and Dadaji, who were waiting for me in the drawing room; I bowed down to seek their blessings. Then, cuddled my sis, Bipasha and asked her to look after everyone and herself. Maa, bought packets of some homemade savories from the kitchen and packed it in my bag. I hugged her tight. Then, came my Baba's turn to seek blessings, when he came out from his room with a packed bag. We were surprised by his act, when he said-

"Natasha, I'm coming with you to Mumbai. Your mother informed me that you are shifting back to the Ladies hostel. I'll help you out; don't worry."

"Baba…I'll manage."

"No! I'm coming along. You will have a lot of stuff to shift."

"Come on, let's go. We have to purchase a ticket for me, too. Last moment will be a problem. My friend is a TT, he said, he will do the needful."

I pulled my phone out from my purse and booked a taxi for us. We left home. On our way, I checked my messages, when I got Karthik's message, which read- *"Hi, Baby! I'm sorry for not replying to your message. I was confused as to how to react; and was busy at the customs office. Will explain once we meet. When are you back from your native place? Call me once you reach Mumbai, till then I will be staying with my dad, at his mansion. I have a surprise for you; bye, my Pookie, love you."*

I showed the message to Baba. He just nodded. Then, said-

"Let's finish your shift to the ladies' hostel, first; then, you message him. Don't spill the beans about my presence at the café."

After travelling approximately 33 hours by train to Mumbai, we hired a taxi and headed straight to Karthik's Apartment. I always have the spare key with me. We entered the apartment and kept our belongings in the hall. I walked to the kitchen and brought a glass of water for Baba. Then, we ordered food for ourselves. Meanwhile, Baba had a glimpse of the apartment. He liked the view from our bedroom towards the sea; which was dark, windy and surrounded with sounds of erratic waves. "Silence is bliss over here." He spoke. He, then, strode towards me and said- "Natasha, the apartment is beautiful and the society looks posh. Karthik, seems to be a rich business man's son."

"Yes, Baba! He is the famous Diamond Merchant, "The Suraj Batliwalla's son."

I got my suitcases from the storage room and started packing my belongings. Baba helped me too. Then, we had our dinner and dozed off. I made Baba sleep in the guest room.

The next morning, I got ready for my college and Baba too got ready to shift my belongings to the ladies' hostel, with the address shared by me. He hired a taxi and started loading it. I hired another taxi and proceeded to the college.

I met Kavita at the administration office and narrated the whole story. She offered her help in shifting; but I informed her that Baba has accompanied me this time to Mumbai, for shifting purposes.

"Nat! That's really sad. Karthik should have thought about you and your needs. Do you need any help in shifting?"

"No, Kavi! Thanks. Baba has come with me this time, to help me shift."

“Oh. Okay. Let me know if you need anything.”

“Yeah. Sure. Bye.”

I left the college by evening, after completing a few formalities. I reached the Ladies hostel and met my father at the lobby; with my belongings, waiting for me. He has completed the payment formalities too; I came to know about it when he shared the receipt with me.

I carried my luggage to the room allotted. While I was settling and setting my things, I received a call from Karthik. I answered his call.

“Hello. Nat! Are you back? Where are you? I just saw Kavita; and she informed me about your arrival. Can you come to our café in an hour? I have a surprise for you.”

“Hmm...Okay.”

I hung up his call; came down to the lobby; and informed Baba about Karthik’s call.

“He called me. We have to go to the café.”

He nodded and we left to the mentioned place. Multiple thoughts about the future were juggling in my mind, while we were on our drive.

At the Café

I reached the place and walked past my steps towards the entrance; while Baba followed me walking at a slower pace. I encountered Karthik seated in our regular place, near the big window. I walked towards him and called out his name. Baba too, settled in a place, diagonally, to that of ours, to be able to hear out all our conversations.

"Karthik. Why have you called me here, all of a sudden?"

"Hi, Nat! You look great today. Here, have some water and cool down first."

A Stewart had got our regular order, on our table, as Karthik had ordered it, prior. *Chocolate truffle cake, cold coffee and a Paneer wrap.* Once he left, I unzipped my bag, and brought out the apartment key.

"Karthik, I have vacated the apartment with all my belongings; and here's the key, I no longer require it. I have shifted back to the Ladies' hostel."

"What? What's wrong Natasha? Just because I didn't reply to your message you have gone to this extent?"

"No, Karthik... It's not only about the message, it's about my future. You are not sure about us, then, on what basis should I live with you?"

"Please, Nat! Don't do this. I love you. I have my own reason for not ruining our relationship because of marriage."

"How on this earth will a relationship get ruined, due to a marriage?" I confronted him.

My Baba heard all our conversations, silently; while, an elderly man got off from his place and reached out to us. The moment I saw him, I had recognized him to be Karthik's dad. I would stalk Karthik, on his social media account, before; and had seen uncle and Karthik in a post.

"Hello, Natasha beta! Sorry, to interrupt. I'm Karthik's father."

"Hello, uncle. I'm acquainted with you."

"But you are meeting him for the first time, isn't it, Nat?" Interrogated Karthik; while uncle too looked amused.

"I used to stalk Karthik on his social media account, after getting acquainted with him."

Karthik's father grinned looking at his son. Then he said- "Natasha, my son is serious about his relationship with you.

Today, I have accompanied him to seek your hand for marriage with my son."

"Uncle…" I was stunned on hearing this. I looked at Karthik, and he approved of the words by nodding his head in agreement.

"Natasha, I had made a few mistakes in my past; for which my wife, and Karthik's mother had to leave us. Thus, Karthik disbelieves in marriage. He doesn't want to lose you; hence, wants to go with the flow in life. Now that I have convinced him, he is ready to make you his D*ulhaniy*a (Bride). Can you please share your parents' number? I want to seek their daughter's hand for marriage with my son.

On hearing this, my Baba couldn't resist, henceforth, rushed to the spot, and soon became the part of the conversation.

"Hello, sir! I'm Natasha's father. I have accompanied her from Kolkata; for emotional support and also to help her shift from Karthik's apartment; as she has decided to do so. I have heard all your conversations; and I am happy and well- convinced to make Karthik as my *Damadh (*Son-in-law). I do understand the reason behind his disapproval for marriage; but as you have come all the way to convince my daughter, I'm really honored for the love and respect you have bestowed on her. Thank you."

“Hello, sir! Glad to meet you.”

“Now that we are all together; let’s decide the date for the marriage.” Announced uncle with a glee.

“Uncle. A minute please. Before you all get engrossed with further arrangements of our marriage; I have a request.”

“Yes, my child! Go ahead.”

“I need at least a year of my time to start my boutique and make it work mode before marriage.”

“That you can do it after marriage too, who’s going to stop you?”

“I’m sure Karthik too needs space and time to settle in life; though he will be joining your business; but he wants to be a self-reliant person.”

“Yes, Dad! Natasha is right.” Said Karthik, standing beside; keeping his arm on my shoulder.

“Okay, then. As you wish.”

Karthik ordered cassata ice-cream for all of us to rejoice at the moment. Once the order reached our place, Karthik, shamelessly spoke out loud in front of our fathers’.

“Natasha and Cassata; I love you both.”

Everyone at our table burst out with a good loud laugh, while I sat there feeling awkward. Later, I too couldn't stop, I laughed out with happy tears rolling down my cheeks.

Baba, left us to make a call to my mother; to inform about my marriage proposal.

Meanwhile, Karthik's father had gone to the counter to pay the bill, when Karthik said- "Now, that we are going to be officially husband and wife soon, let's get your belongings back to our apartment, Nat"

"No, Karthik. I will stay in the Ladies' hostel only, until our marriage date. Let's make a deal that-Weekends, we will meet for sure; no matter what; and I will stay there with you."

"What is this, Nat? Why are you so adamant?"

"It's not being adamant, baby! My dad has just paid the full amount. I'm sure our love is not so weak that it has to be dependent. Most of us have misconstrued love. If we love one another, then, we must live together otherwise our love is weak. I used to think in the same manner; but after some space between us, I realized that, Love teaches us to be stronger, along with loyalty and understanding; despite the distance."

"Okay, Shona! No man in this world has won from their wife in an argument. You are right and always will be."

"Shona? You have learnt a Bengali word. Wow!"

"Yes, just for you, my Pookie."

I gave a pat on Karthik's arm and he pulled me closer for a hug. While the entire room with guests at the café had their eyes hooked on us.

Our parents left us alone to their respective destinations. Baba booked his tickets and left Mumbai; Uncle proceeded to his mansion; and Karthik gave me a lift to the ladies' hostel; playing all our favorite 90s songs; which we used to hear on our drive. We GenZs are bizarre in nature. Lifestyle should be GenZ, but, expectation for love, to be like 90s.

The Wedding

In a year, since the time we met our respective parents; lots of things changed in our lives. I got engrossed with my boutique; Karthik too travelled a lot for business purposes. But he always made it during the weekends as per our deal. We attended many marriages together; some were of our respective friends and few were mutual friends. A few marriages were held in the Mosque; some at the Church; and many at the Temples, along with a grand Reception. But, when it was our turn to get married, Karthik and I met in our apartment for the discussion. We had a group conference call, inviting Karthik's father and my parents, and decided the wedding date to be held on 14th February 2026.

My parents had asked Uncle about the custom to be followed at the wedding, when he said- "Let's have a Bengali style wedding at our mansion. Reception to be in a Western theme, at a grand hotel, in Mumbai; while, the Puja, Mehndi ceremony, and Haldi ceremony will be held at your place, at Kolkata. Karthik and I, will join you all. I will inform Karthik's mother to join the gathering; but can't confirm. Cocktail party is on me and to be held at our mansion."

“That’s a great Plan Uncle. Thank you.”

My parents and grandparents, who were on the call; and were hearing our conversations, were pleased with the decision.

Baba spoke as a responsible father- “Sir, how many guests are you expecting at the wedding? Please, share the count.”

“Samdhi Ji...Sir, mat pukariye, please.” (In India, it’s the culture to summon ‘In-laws’ of both sides as Samdhi).

“Samdhi Ji... You don’t have to take the burden, it’s my kind request. We shall share the expenses starting from Puja to the Reception Party. Cocktail party is from my end, totally.

“Okay, Samdhi Ji. Thank you.”

Finally, the day had arrived, where it was our last day of our relationship, as GF and BF. Since, the next day, all the ceremonies were lined up, till we officially got married. We were nervous and happy too. It was like a Cocktail – where the alcohol gets mixed with varied flavor syrups in one glass. Similarly, we were given to one another eternally, under the glass of marriage, mixed with excitement, nervousness, fatigue, and sleep deprivation. Love and its misconstrued theory have been cleared by our experienced elders of our home. I’m lucky to have been born in a family where three generations lived together under one roof, experiencing different mindset towards life and its journey. It was Uncle's efforts that Karthik and I are going to be together. Good parenting is really required in our generation and for the upcoming generations.

On 14th February 2026, we got married. The next day, we got our marriage registered at the Sub- Registrar's Office.

I have already made it clear to Uncle and Karthik before the marriage, that I will not change my surname after marriage, it will remain Natasha Chatterjee only; and they being too generous agreed to it. After a month; Karthik and I resumed our respective work. We lived in the mansion and not in our Worli Apartment; as Uncle...Oops! Papaji... Was living alone in a big mansion; and due to his age and ailments, he needed someone, who can look after him. Though 24 hours assistance was hired, still, the Family gives happiness and support; and Karthik being the only son, and I, being the *Bahu (*Daughter-in-Law), have to fulfill our duties and responsibilities.

Author - Pratima Raj

"The Journey from a home maker to an Author makes her glorify her roots and the route."

Pratima Raj has authored four books entitled- "Cocktales", "Virgin Mother", "The Colostrum" & " Love Misconstrued"

She is a M.phil graduate in English. She has augmented her skills by procuring a Diploma course in Creative Writing. She has also procured a degree in Business Management. She is a certified Your Quote writer and has penned more than 3500 quotes. She has published her quote book entitled, "Enchanting Words of Mind," and has been a co- author for six anthologies. She has a blog, named- "Magic In Words."

She has won "Inspiring Indian Awards" in the genre of Literature, awarded by the "Spectrum of Thoughts."

She has conducted a workshop- "Magic In Words", on creative writing skills in one of the esteemed education institution in Coimbatore.

Apart from penning stories, quote and poem, she shares her interest in reading books of different genre.

She shows inquisitiveness in exploring and experiencing novel opportunities which leads to self- development and hence her author journey was accomplished only because of her passion, determination and consistency.

Books By Pratima Raj

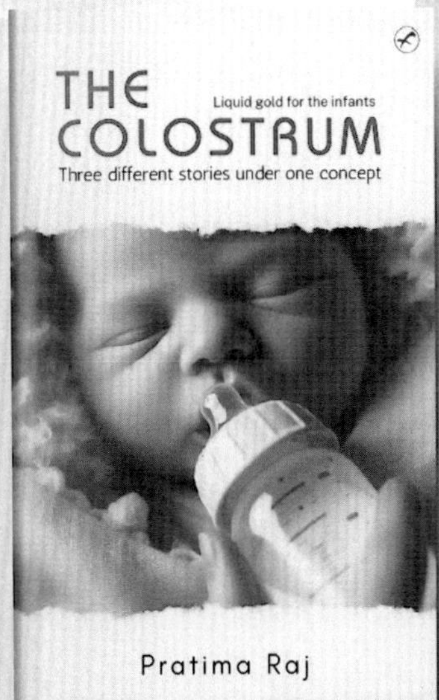